For Jo and Roy Peace
—B.D.

To Phil,
Many thanks
—A.B.

Text copyright © 1988 by Berlie Doherty
Illustrations copyright © 1999 by Alison Bartlett
This American edition 1999 published by Orchard Books
This edition published in Great Britain in 1999 by Hodder Children's Books
Published by arrangement with Hodder Children's Books

Berlie Doherty and Alison Bartlett assert the moral right
to be identified as the author and illustrator of this work.

Orchard Books, A Grolier Company
95 Madison Avenue, New York, NY 10016

Printed in Hong Kong. The text of this book is set in 21 point Goudy.
The illustrations are acrylic paintings.
1 3 5 7 9 10 8 6 4 2

Library of Congress Cataloging-in-Publication Data
Doherty, Berlie.
Paddiwak and Cozy / by Berlie Doherty; illustrated by Alison Bartlett. p. cm.
Summary: When Sally brings home a new cat, her old cat, Paddiwak, hisses and storms off into the night.
ISBN 0-531-30180-X (trade : alk. paper)
[1. Cats—Fiction. 2. Jealousy—Fiction.] I. Bartlett, Alison, ill. II. Title.
PZ7.D6947Pad 1999 [E]—dc21 98-46168

Paddiwak and Cozy

by
Berlie Doherty

illustrated by
Alison Bartlett

Orchard Books • New York

Paddiwak
is a prince of a cat,
a heartthrob (quite a snob),
very smart in his neat black suit
and his little white shirt
and socks.

All day long,
he sits in the sun
and washes himself
with his sticky-lick tongue.

But yesterday was a terrible day.
Sally came home with a big blue box,
a box that bumped and shivered and shook,
a box with noisy feet inside.

Paddiwak yawned and slid off his chair.
He sniffed at the box with the noisy feet.
The lid flipped up, and out came a whisker
and two and three and four and more . . .

. . . of another cat.
But what a cat!
A laugh of a cat,
a dumpling cat

with a black bit here
and a white bit there,
floppy round
the tummy and
great big paws.

Sally said, "Here you are, Paddiwak, a friend for you."
Paddiwak hissed and arched his back,
fluffed up his tail, and spit-spit-spat . . .

ran through his cat flap
out in the rain.
"I'm never, never, never going home again!"

The new cat ran to the fireplace.
She climbed up the chimney in great distress.
When Sally pulled her down,
she had soot on her face.

Paddiwak crawled under
the garden shed.
"I'm never, never, never
going home," he said.

The new cat hid
in the sewing box
and made a secret nest
of wool and rags.

Paddiwak climbed up
the apple tree.
"I'm never, never, never
going home," said he.

The new cat ran upstairs,
lost and scared,

squeezing under dusty beds
and sneezing there.

Paddiwak howled
on the garden wall.
"I'm never, never, never
going home at all."

The new cat found the cellar, dark as dreams,
and tiptoed round the shadows,
where she couldn't be seen,
and cried in the corners all alone.
And Sally cried too.
"I used to have one cat,
I thought I'd have two,
and now I've lost them both.

I've lost my little slim cat,
my heartthrob, my quite a snob,
and I've lost my new cuddly cat,
my laugh of a cat, my crazy cat.
I thought I'd have two cats,
and now I've got none!"

When all the house
was sleeping,
the new cat crept up
the cellar steps.

She had soot on her face,
wool on her tail, fluff on her fur,
a cobweb on her whiskers,
and her feet were filthy.
"I'm a mess!"

She climbed into the linen cupboard,
warm as a pocket, secret as a whisper,
and purred herself to sleep.

When outside was too dark
and cold and wet for anything,
Paddiwak pushed open his cat flap.
"I'll just come in to hide from the rain,
but as soon as it stops I'll run away again."

His fur dripped
muddy puddles up the stairs.
He had twigs in his tail
and leaves round his ears,
and his socks were
black as boots,
but he didn't care.

He found his favorite den,
the linen cupboard.
He could hardly climb in,
he was so cold and tired.
He heaved himself up
and found . . .

something as cuddly
as a cushion
to lay his head on,
something as comfy as slippers
to warm his feet by.

"Mmm! Cozy!" he sighed.
"Ah! Paddiwak!" Cozy purred.

And next morning,
they licked each other clean.